D0590306
700028633443

lauren child

We honestly CAN look after your dog

PUFFIN

Text based on script written by Bridget Hurst and Carol Noble

Illustrations from the TV animation produced by Tiger Aspect

PUFFIN BOOKS
Published by the Penguin Group: London, New York, Ireland, Australia, Canada, India, New Zealand and South Africa
Penguin Books Ltd, Registered Offices: 80 Strand, London WC2R 0RL, England

www.penguin.com

First published 2005
3 5 7 9 10 8 6 4

Made and printed in Italy
ISBN-13: 978-0-14138-210-4
ISBN-10: 0-141-38210-4

I have this little sister Lola.
She is small and very funny.
At the moment Lola really, really wants to have a dog.
But Mum and Dad say she can't because our flat
is too small and Lola is too young to look after it.

Lola says,
"Say woof, Charlie."

So I say,
"Woof."

Then Lola says, "Sit!"

So I sit.

My cereal bowl is now a dog bowl.

And she has made me a **dog** bed.

Lola just loves **dogs**.

A lot.

One day we went to the park.

There was me and my friend Marv,
Lola and her friend Lotta.
And Sizzles.
Sizzles is Marv's dog.

Lola loves Sizzles.

So does Lola's best friend, Lotta.

Lola says, "You ask."
Lotta says, "No you."

So Lola says,
"Marv, can we look after Sizzles?"

Marv says,
"Lola, do you know
about dogs?"

Lola says,
"Yes I do. Everything."

And Lotta says, "So do I."

Lola says,
"We know that Sizzles
is a very extremely very clever dog.
And we know he can do really very good tricks."
Lotta says, "And if he wanted he could absolutely roll over."

Lola says, "And juggle. All sorts of things."

Lotta says,
"And paint pictures.
And speak English."

Lola says,
"And
walk
on
two
legs.

And dance.
Definitely, I think.
Lotta, do you know
I think
Sizzles
can do
really
anything."

Marv says,
"Sizzles is the
cleverest dog ever,
anywhere.
Watch
this.

"Sizzles. Sit,
Sizzles!
Sit!

Sit!

Sit,

Sizzles?"

While Marv is trying to
make Sizzles sit, I see some of our
friends playing football
and I think I'd really like to play too.

So I say,
"We could play just one game,
Marv?"

Marv says,
"But who is going to look after
Sizzles?"

Lola says, "Me!"

Lotta says, "Me!"

I say,
"It's only for a little while.
He'll be OK with Lola and Lotta.
I'm pretty sure he will."

So Marv says,
"OK.
But you do know
there are lots of rules
if you want to
look after Sizzles.

No chocolates.

No cakes.

And
no sweets
of any kind.

Completely
no digging...

and

no chasing birds.

And

no splashing

in
puddles.

And definitely NO taking him off the lead."

Marv says,
"Do you honestly promise to
look after my dog?"

Lola says, "Honestly,
we do promise honestly,
to look after your dog."

Lotta says,
"Honestly and promisedly, we do,
to look after your dog."

Lola says,
"Dogs must be stroked and patted."

Lotta says,
"To tell them we're their friend.

Lola says,
"Playing is...
what makes dogs happy."

Lotta says,
"And grooming makes dogs feel pretty."

Lola says,
"Dogs must go outside
and must walk."

Lotta says,
"Otherwise what is the point
of their legs?"

Then Lola says,
"Lotta, I don't think you really know
all about dogs like me."

And Lotta says,
"Lola, I really do know
everything about dogs."

Lola says, "But Lotta, I'm in charge."

And Lotta says,
"So am I."

Lola says,
"We're both in charge, but I think that Mary said that I was a little bit more in charge than you.

You see, Lotta, you must hold the lead like this. See?" Lotta says, "Oh no, Lola. Really you must do it like this."

"Ooops!"

"Sizzles, where are you?"

"Where are you, Sizzles?"

"Sizzles,
where
are
you?"

Lola says,
"Do you think we have
lost him **forever**?"

Lotta says,
"I think he was **sad** actually."

Then Lola says...

But then Lola says,
"Oh no! There are two Sizzleses!"

And Lotta says,
"No, Lola, there are two dogs.
But only one is Sizzles."

Lola says,
"But which one?"

Lotta says,
"I don't know."

Lola says,
"The clever one!
Sizzles can do anything, remember?"

Lotta says, "Yes. Sizzles can do anything."

Lola says, "Sizzles can sit!"

Then Lotta says,
"Sizzles! Sit. Sit. Sit!"

And Lola says,
"Sit. Sit. Sit!"

Lotta says,
"Sit, sit, sit,
sit!"

Then Lola says,
"Look! It must be Sizzles.
He's sitting!"

And Lola says, "But Sizzles would never get lost."
Lotta says, "No, he's a very extremely very clever dog."
Lola says, "He can do anything."
And Lotta says, "He can do absolutely anything."